To the actual selfless and talented treehouse builders.
And also for Dad and Charlie.
—T.S.

For Avalon Skye and Faedra Blue,
who build much magic and possibility every day
—D.L.

For Leo, my diligent collector of stray sticks and leaves
—N.S.

Visit us on the Web! randomhousekids.com

Educators and librarians, for a variety of teaching tools, visit us at RHTeachersLibrarians.com

Library of Congress Cataloging-in-Publication Data
Names: Surratt, Tereasa, author. | Lukas, Donna, author.
Title: The forever tree / by Tereasa Surratt and Donna Lukas ; illustrations by Nicola Slater.
Description: New York : Crown Books for Young Readers, [2018] | Summary: "When a beloved tree gets sick,
the human and animal communities work together to give it a new life." —Provided by publisher.
Identifiers: LCCN 2017014874 (print) | LCCN 2017022931 (ebook) | ISBN 978-0-553-52392-8 (hardcover) |
ISBN 978-0-553-52393-5 (hardcover library edition) | ISBN 978-0-553-52394-2 (ebook)
Subjects: | CYAC: Trees—Fiction.
Classification: LCC PZ7.1.S876 (ebook) | LCC PZ7.1.S876 Fo 2008 (print) | DDC [E]—dc23

Book design by Nicole de las Heras

MANUFACTURED IN CHINA
10 9 8 7 6 5 4 3 2 1
First Edition

The FOREVER TREE

Tereasa Surratt *and* Donna Lukas

Illustrated by Nicola Slater

Crown Books for Young Readers ♔ New York

This is a true story about a Tree that grew
from something more than water and sunshine.
It grew from love.

The Animals knew the Tree was very special, which is why they held all their sleepovers, weddings and championship bingo tournaments inside.

They fed the Tree with laughter, singing and dancing. And from its deepest roots to its highest branches, that's how the Tree grew strong and tall and proud.

The Raccoons were in charge of keeping the Tree neat and tidy. They carefully cleaned it every day with gentle paws.

The Squirrels stocked the Tree with books and games and colorful party supplies.

The Chipmunks adored the Tree, too. But they were often distracted by the shapes of clouds and thoughts of chestnuts, so none of their chores ever really got done.

For years, the Animals had the Tree all to themselves.
So very many surprise birthday parties, first kisses and
Secret Squirrel Social Scout Meetings happened there.

One day, an Unexpected Visitor arrived.

A Grandfather. He was a strong and tall and proud man.

He knew the Tree was special, too. He threw a rope up and over
its sturdiest limb. His hands worked quickly and with love.

The next morning, a little girl named Charlie came out to play.
She saw the swing her Grandfather had made just for her.
"Thank you, Grandfather!" said Charlie. "Push me! Push me! Please!"

The Raccoons, Squirrels and Chipmunks all stopped
what they were doing. People had never noticed their
special Tree before.

And from the Grandfather's act of love, something
new and beautiful began to grow.

Every day, Charlie's Grandfather pushed
her on the swing. Soon more Children came.

They brought their Mothers, Fathers, Grandmothers and Grandfathers. They pumped their legs and voices up to the sky.

At first, the Animals were worried. Maybe even a little annoyed.

This was *their* special Tree. They weren't quite sure they wanted to share it.

The Raccoons began plotting a revolution underground.

The Squirrels argued for Animal and People Togetherness.

The Chipmunks were not of much help at all because they were still gazing at the clouds.

But the People turned out to be good neighbors. They were kind to the Animals and their beloved Tree. They shared their most delicious snacks.

The Raccoons advised the Animals, "Be nice and don't bite."

The swinging went on for many days. For months and years.

There were more graduation picnics, polka parties and hide-and-seek contests than you could count on all your paws. There was always love and laughter.

And it kept the Tree growing strong, tall and proud.

But one Spring after a Long Hard Winter, the Tree did not wake up with budding leaves.

The Tree did not wake up at all.

That Spring, Grandfather did not return, either.

Oh, how Charlie and the Raccoons, Squirrels and Chipmunks cried.

Then Official People came and said
the Tree was now Unsafe.

The Animals didn't know what this meant. They felt afraid.

The Raccoons organized an emergency meeting. They had heard of People who knew how to fix things, People who knew how to use their hearts and brains and hands to make things that last forever, special People who believed that something beautiful is always worth saving.

The Animals began their search.
The Raccoons identified Architects by poking inside
their recycling bins.

The Squirrels found Carpenters by following the
scent of wood. They whispered in their sleeping ears.

The Chipmunks lured Artists with trails of chestnuts and wild red berries arranged in impossibly intricate swirls.

Planners and Builders of all kinds were found.

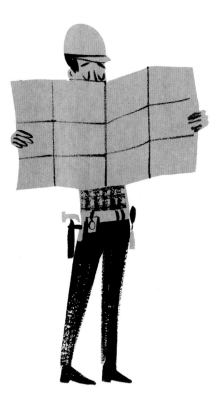

Together, they came up with an idea to save the Tree. They thought, sketched and measured.

They sawed and scurried and sanded.

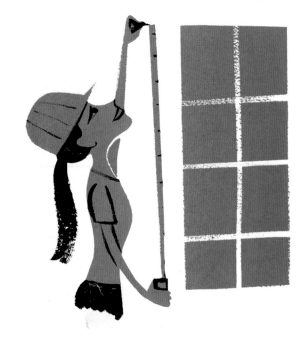

Day and night, they worked quickly, skillfully and with love.

When the Tree House was built, the People and Animals agreed it was the perfect place to hold their most special weddings, sleepovers and championship bingo tournaments.

They promised each other that their Tree would stand forever, strong and tall and proud.

The swing would always hang from its sturdiest limb.

And somewhere, way, way, way up above, the Grandfather looked down and smiled.

Author's Note

Photo courtesy of Tereasa Surratt

IN 2004, TEREASA SURRATT AND HER husband, David, purchased the Camp Wandawega property—an old Wisconsin campground where David spent many years as a boy. To celebrate the event, Tereasa's father, Tom, hung a rope swing on a large elm tree at the center of the camp.

A year and a half after breaking ground on the land, Tom passed. Not long after that, the tree contracted Dutch elm disease.

Word of the tree's plight spread, inspiring local artists, many of whom were strangers to the Surratt family, to contribute their time and effort to give the tree a second life. Almost all of the components used in the converted tree house came from recycled or reclaimed materials, including the tree itself, whose trunk was healthy enough to be used as the centerpiece of the structure.

The three-story cottage, named Tom's Tree-house in honor of Tereasa's father, has gained national media attention. And the rope swing still hangs proudly on the tree today.

You can visit Tom's Treehouse and Camp Wandawega online at wandawega.com, or in person in Elkhorn, Wisconsin.

Photo courtesy of Bob Coscarelli